The Adventures of EDISON MATTHEWS

Written and Illustrated by **MATT GEILER**

SP

SICK PICNIC

PRESS

LOS ANGELES   OMAHA   CHICAGO   NEW YORK

For information regarding permission, please write to:
Permissions Department
Sick Picnic Media
6720 S 185th Ave
Omaha, Nebraska 68135

Sick Picnic Press and associated logos are trademarks
and/or registered trademarks of Sick Picnic Media, LLC.

ISBN-10: 0-9978457-0-8   ISBN-13: 978-0-9978457-0-9
2 3 4 5 6 7 8 9 10   10 9 8 7 6 5 4 3 2
Printed in the United States
First printing, August 2016

THE ADVENTURES of EDISON MATTHEWS

For Edison, my first greatest adventure.

EDISON MATTHEWS was **bored**.

The morning was **slow** and **sluggish** and **gloomy** and **glummish** and made Edison want to stay in his pajamas.

He was even tired of video games.

"I don't know what to do with myself," Edison sighed, **flopping** onto the couch.

"You could play outside," his dad suggested.

"But it's going to rain and I hate being outside in the rain because it feels like **worms** and **spiders** are dancing on my neck."

His father could tell he was really, truly bored. Edison heaved another sigh. "I'm DOOMED," he muttered.

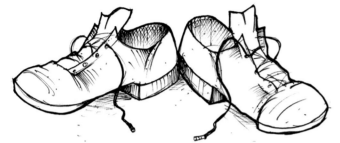

"How do worms and spiders dance?" wondered his dad.

Edison unflopped himself from the couch.

"Well, worms wiggle," he said.

"And spiders tickle-tap when they walk."

"Let's try it," his dad winked.

Edison and his dad spider-tapped and worm-wiggled until they were laughing so hard they had to stop.

"You have a very powerful imagination," chuckled his father. "When I'm bored, I use my imagination to visit other places."

"Like taking a trip in your mind?" Edison asked.

"You can travel anywhere. All you have to do is close your eyes. Where would you go?"

"To **AFRICA** on a purple rhinoceros!" whooped Edison.

"My very own safari! And nobody else would be riding a purple rhino."

"They're extremely rare," agreed his dad.

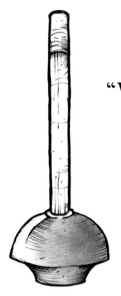

"We'd go deep into the JUNGLE," Edison continued. "But I'd make sure to take a plunger because of all the wild animals."

"Why a plunger?"

"If anything tries to eat you, you can suck its face right off its head," declared Edison. "And it's good to have if the toilet gets stopped up."

"The jungle has very suspect plumbing," nodded his father.

"Sometimes I imagine I'm a **ballet** DANCER," said Edison.

"That's different than worm-wiggling. You float your arms and legs like they're made of glass. The dancers wear puffy flowers around their waists. And the best ballerinas are always rushing."

"Do you mean Russian?" clarified his dad.

"That's what I said. They're always hurrying because it's cold in those tights."

"Especially in Moscow," his father conceded.

"My teacher told us about a mountain where the gods live," Edison remembered. "It's so high the top is covered in clouds."

"Yes, it's called OLYMPUS."

Edison imagined sitting on a gleaming throne in the sky, eating flavored ice fresh from the clouds, and living forever.

"If I was a god, I'd stay home from school most days."

"But sometimes you'd show up?" his dad asked.

"One or two days," explained Edison. "I wouldn't want to get in trouble with the teacher. I'd miss recess."

Edison thought of a dream he always had. In it, he was soaring skyward with a flock of geese. As he flew, he could feel the air slide over him like a feathery blanket.

"What are you imagining now?" his father asked softly.

"Flying with the geese," exhaled Edison. "I wish I really could FLY. It feels so nice in my dream."

"What else do you wish you could do?"

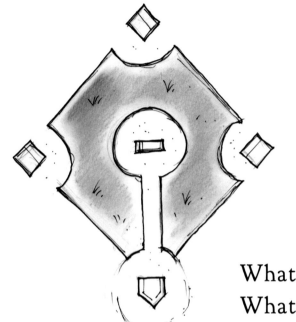

"I wish I could throw a baseball so fast nobody could hit it," Edison pined. "On TV they call it

'throwing SMOKE.'

What if I could throw it so fast the ball really *did* smoke? What if it lit on fire?"

"You'd literally be bringing the heat," Edison's dad joked, slapping his knees and chortling a fake laugh. "Get it? Fire? Heat?"

Edison didn't think it was *that* hilarious.

"Anything else?" asked his dad.

"I can also imagine myself as a cowboy," Edison said.

"I wanted to be a Wild West gunslinger when I was a little boy, too," his father echoed.

"But I wouldn't shoot people," added Edison. "They'd be so afraid of my sneer that I could drink

all the ROOT BEER I want."

"You're the roughest, toughest hombre I've ever seen in these parts," drawled his dad. "Unfortunately, we're fresh out of root beer."

"Dad, do you ever imagine doing things you're afraid of in real life?"

"Absolutely," his dad replied. "Usually those things involve clients."

"Sometimes I imagine that

all the MONSTERS I'm afraid of

in real life are actually afraid of me."

"You're much braver than I am," shivered his dad. "Some of my clients are cousins of the Werewolf."

Edison gazed at the Christmas lights hanging over his dad's desk. He squinted his eyes until the little bulbs became twinkling stars of red, blue, and green.

"What do you see?"

"A whole fog of magical. fairies dancing in the air," whispered Edison. "They live in a secret cave where they guard their treasure."

"What treasure are they guarding?" his father whispered back.

"Little cheesecakes," breathed Edison. "Like the kind Mom keeps in the freezer."

"I'm getting hungry," his dad hankered. "How does a cheeseburger sound?"

"Yay! Cheeseburgers!" sang Edison. "Can we stop at the bookstore while we're out?"

"Books and burgers," nodded his dad. "A classic combo."

"I love smelling the pages," Edison giggled. "I imagine BOOKS growing from TREES.

And book farmers pick them and bring them to the store. Like apples."

"Only the freshest books get picked!" laughed his dad.

In the car, Edison smiled thinking of his imagination adventures. The day was no longer gloomy and glum. Best of all, Edison wasn't bored anymore.

"Our imaginations are like rockets, aren't they, Dad?"

"They'll take us ANYWHERE we want TO GO."

"But I'm already where I want to go," yawned Edison.

"And where's that?" his dad asked.

"Right here with you."

Neither of them could  imagine ANYTHING

better.